For Olive, Cherry & Ivy, who I could never get to sleep!

Published in the UK by Scholastic Children's Books, 2020
Euston House, 24 Eversholt Street, London, NW1 1DB

Scholastic Ltd Ireland offices at: Unit 89E, Lagan Road,
Dublin Industrial Estate, Glasnevin, Dublin 11.

A division of Scholastic Limited
London ~ New York ~ Toronto ~ Sydney ~ Auckland
Mexico City ~ New Delhi ~ Hong Kong

SCHOLASTIC and associated logos are trademarks
and/or registered trademarks of Scholastic Inc.

Text © Matt Carr, 2021
Illustrations © Matt Carr, 2021

The right of Matt Carr to be identified as the author
and illustrator of this work has been asserted by him
under the Copyright, Designs and Patents Act 1988.

ISBN 978 07023 0623 5

Printed in Italy by L.E.G.O S.p.A

Papers used by Scholastic Children's Books are
made from wood grown in sustainable forests.

10 9 8 7 6 5 4 3 2 1

www.scholastic.co.uk

■■SCHOLASTIC

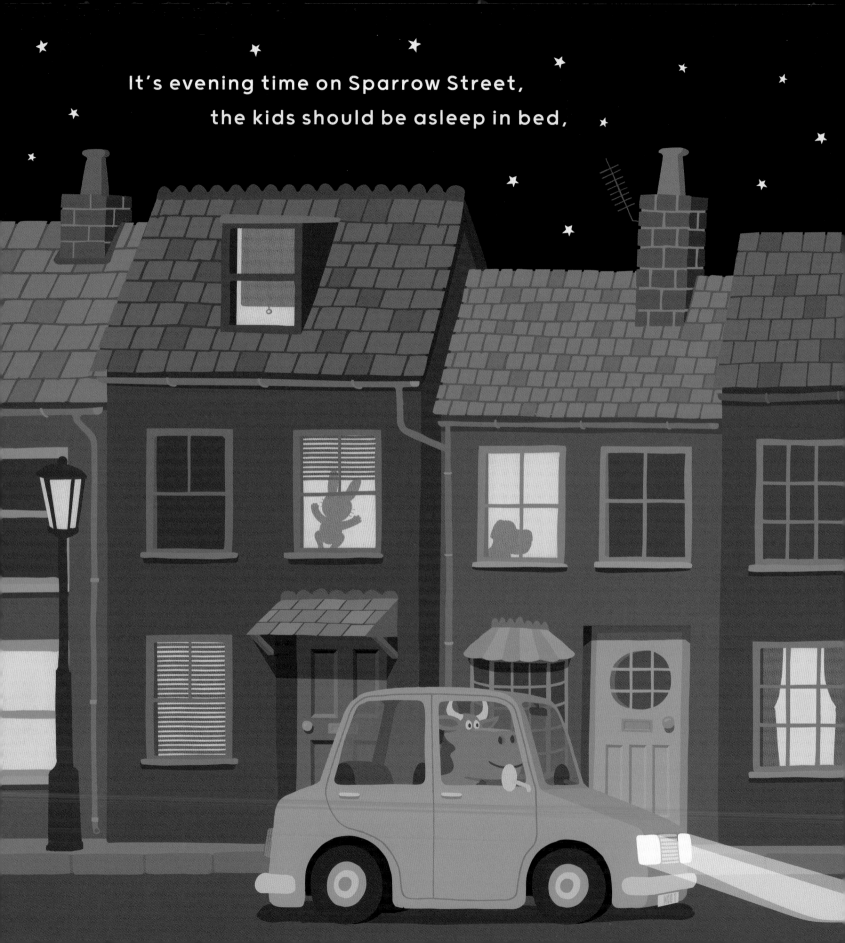

It's evening time on Sparrow Street,
the kids should be asleep in bed,

but it looks like they are all still up
and doing other things instead.

William Rabbit at number two,
can't stop bouncing around.
He had too much crumble for pudding,
and all that sugar means
he won't calm down.

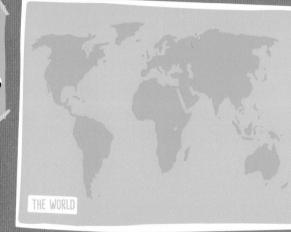

William thinks it's hilarious,
but his mum doesn't
find it that funny.

NOW GO TO SLEEP!

she tells him.
She is NOT
a happy bunny!

Next door, young Kenny the puppy,
is watching that TV show again.
But staring at a screen before bed,
is not very good for his brain.

NOW GO TO SLEEP!

says his dad,
and takes the
tablet away...

...but this doggy's mind
can't unwind
and awake young
Kenny will stay.

Up the road at number five,
Mrs Bear kisses Mabel goodnight.

NOW GO TO SLEEP!

she says,
and switches
off the light.

But Mabel is scared of the dark,
so she hides under the cover.
Night time noises keep her awake,
she wants a cuddle from her mother.

They're not the only kids who aren't in the land of nod.

Coco is reading her comic book, another member of the wide-awake squad.

Delilah is still in the bathroom. She's in a bit of a rush. But this time it's really not her fault, as she has so many teeth to brush!

By the time everyone's asleep
the hour is very late.
All too soon, they'll need to get up,
school starts at half past eight!

The children are all really tired
in the classroom the very next morning.
But Mrs Moo knows what to do,
to stop everyone from yawning.

I won't be a moment kids,
she says.

I'm just going to get someone.
If she's awake, she'll be able to help
and she's also a lot of fun!

...so when Mrs Moo knocks on her door, you can imagine her surprise.

I'd be happy to help yawns Shirley.

I'll be there right away.

But when Mrs Moo leaves the room, she nods off for the rest of the day!

So here is a little lullaby, to assist with your bedtime habits. It's guaranteed to work for everyone, including bouncy rabbits!

"When you want to drift off to dream land, try listening to soothing songs...

...and if you're afraid of the dark, why not leave a little light on?

"Don't stare at a screen before bed – it will keep your brain wide awake...

...and you'll have trouble nodding off if you've just eaten sweets or cake!"

If you want help with your slumber, you can always count on Shirley Sheep...

And sure enough, later that night...

NOW THEY'VE GONE

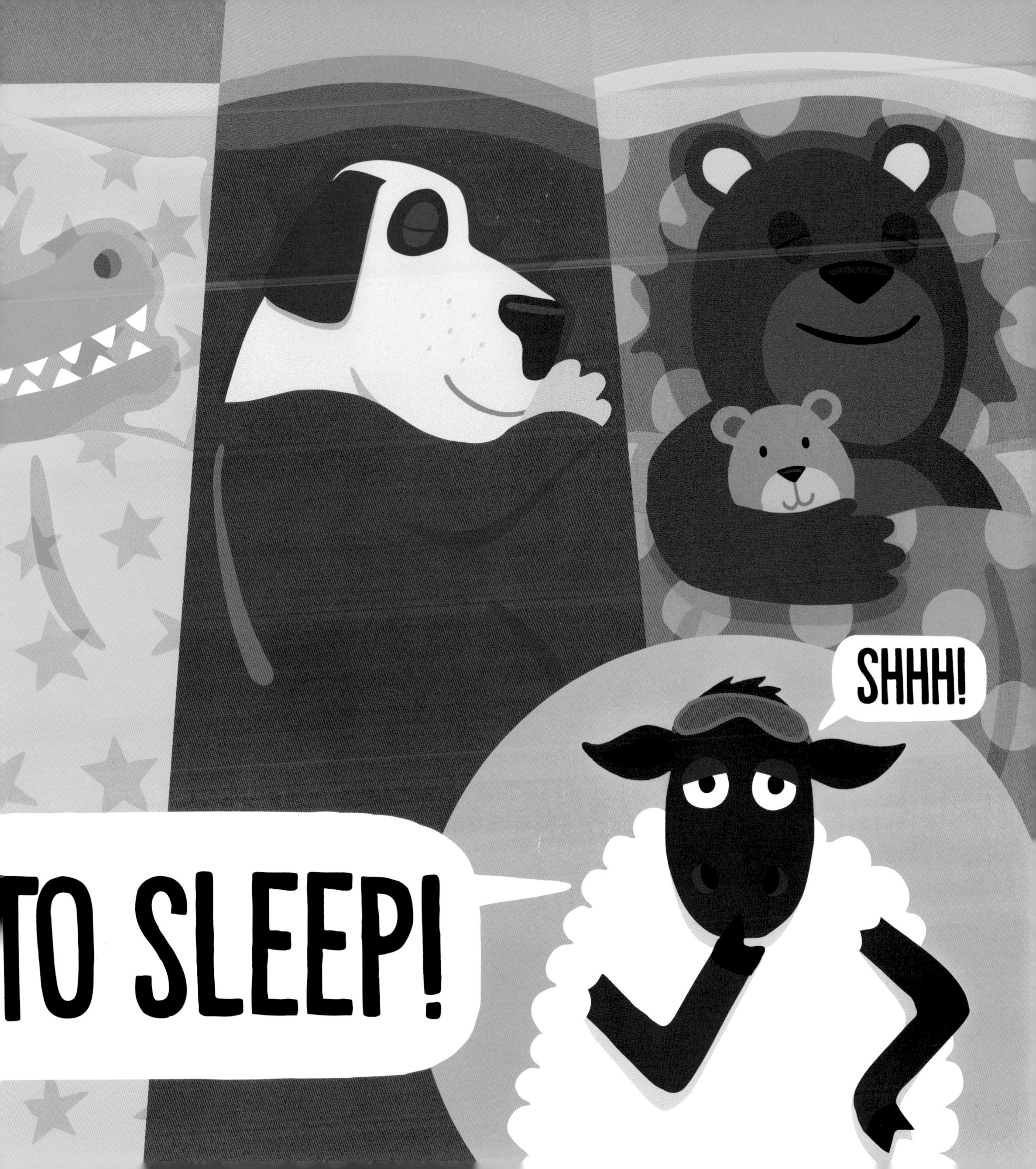
TO SLEEP!
SHHH!

ALL ABOUT SLEEP

with Shirley Sheep

EW BREW

Humans have

FOUR TO SIX DREAMS

every night.

BATS

can sleep up to 20 hours per day.

GIRAFFES

only sleep for about 30 minutes a day in the wild.

HIBERNATION* is what animals do when the weather is bad and food is in short supply. They become inactive to save energy.

YAWN

The animal that hibernates most is the **dormouse**. A dormouse can hibernate for up to 11 months!

*Hibernation is NOT actually sleeping.